I Love You Mary Jane

Lorna Balian

ABINGDON PRESS
Nashville   New York

For Peter, Sarah, Mary, David, Paula, and Joseph

Today is Mary Jane's Birthday Party.

Don't forget.

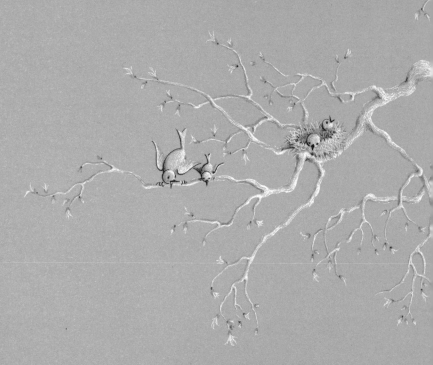

Don't forget about Mary Jane's Birthday!

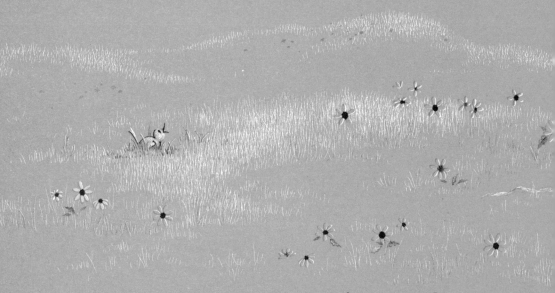

Are you ready for the party?

Did you get a present for Mary Jane?

Don't forget about the party.

There'll be a BIG SURPRISE!

Bring a present!

Why are you just sitting there, Chief?

Today is Mary Jane's Birthday Pow-Wow!

Mary Jane has a surprise for EVERYONE!

You'll like the party!

There'll be a surprise...

and ice cream!

Ice Cream?

I like parties!

Heap
Big
Party!

Tee-Hee!

This is fun! Oh Boy!

I made this
for you . . .
isn't it lovely?

I caught this
special . . . for you.

I love you,
Mary Jane

I Love
Mary Jane

I want
you to have
my beautiful
umbrella.

Here. . . .
You can be
the chief!

It's the best
kind of cake . . .
homemade!

I want to give you
my favorite ribbon.

Happy Birthday to you.
Happy Birthday to you.
Happy Birthday, dear Mary Jane...
Happy Birthday to you!

Oh, thank you,
Mary Jane!

Tee-Hee!

Heap Big Party!

Come back . . . Come back . . . I love you, too!

Thank you, Mary Jane.
You're nice.